(Dec /98)
Merry Christmas Lauren,
Love,
Gramma & Papa

Carol Carrick

Two Very Little Sisters

ILLUSTRATED BY
Erika Weihs

Clarion Books · New York

To Eleanor Olsen

With appreciation to the Dukes County Historical Society and to
Eulalie Reagan of the *Vineyard Gazette* for their help in researching
this story.

Clarion Books • a Houghton Mifflin Company imprint • 215 Park Avenue South, New York, NY 10003
Text copyright © 1993 by Carol Carrick • Illustrations copyright © 1993 by Erika Weihs • All rights
reserved. • For information about permission to reproduce selections from this book, write to Permissions,
Houghton Mifflin Company, 215 Park Avenue South, New York, NY 10003. Printed in the U.S.A.
Library of Congress Cataloging-in-Publication Data
Carrick, Carol. • Two very little sisters / by Carol Carrick; illustrated by Erika Weihs. p. cm. • Summary:
Describes the lives of the two midget sisters who were circus stars for twenty years and who preferred to
be called "little people." • ISBN 0-395-60927-5 • 1. Adams, Lucy—Juvenile literature. 2. Adams, Sarah,
b. 1861—Juvenile literature. 3. Midgets—United States—Biography—Juvenile literature. [1. Adams, Lucy.
2. Adams, Sarah, b. 1861. 3. Midgets.] I. Weihs, Erika, ill. II. Title. CT9992.A33C37 1993
973.8'092—dc20 [B] 91-39123
CIP AC WOZ 10 9 8 7 6 5 4 3 2 1

Once there were two little sisters.
Lucy was born first and then
Sarah came two years later.
Each was perfect in every way,
although they were very small.

Every spring their mother measured them
against the cupboard door.
While their brother and sisters
grew bigger every year,
Lucy and Sarah stayed small,
so small they could walk
under the kitchen table.

Everybody loved the little sisters.
They washed themselves,
they dressed themselves,
and they did their chores.
They were treated like everyone else,
except that their father made them tiny shoes
and their own little chairs
so their toes could reach the floor.

When they were late for school,
the sisters took the short way through a pasture.
They ran past the cows,
who seemed big and frightening
to girls so small.

Lucy and Sarah did well in school
and they had fun at recess.
The other girls begged them to be their baby dolls,
and the boys gave them rides on their shoulders.

Sunday mornings the family rode to church in a wagon.
There the two sisters stood on a chair
to recite their Sunday school lessons.

12

They loved to sit on top of the organ
and sing to the congregation
in their high, sweet voices.

And in the Christmas pageant, they were angels.

In those days, P.T. Barnum was the world's greatest showman.
He read a newspaper story about the sisters,
who were teenagers now.

Barnum wanted them in his circus
because they were so small.
"Come with me," he said, "and I'll make you famous."
The two girls had never thought of leaving home,
but the circus sounded exciting.

Their parents worried.
Could two little sisters take care of themselves
in such a big world?
But Lucy and Sarah wanted to go.
So their father built two little trunks,
their mother packed their clothes,
and the sisters waved good-bye.

The circus traveled the country.
Crowds lined the streets to see the parade.
As the sisters passed by on prancing ponies,
people called, "Look at the midgets!
Aren't they cute!"

But the girls didn't like being stared at
just because they were small.
They didn't like being called midgets, either.
So they left the circus.

Now the two sisters went back to school.
They took dancing lessons.

They took acting lessons.
And they learned how to sing
so their small voices could fill a great hall.

The sisters performed in towns
throughout the Wild West.
Soon they became a big success.
But traveling by train and coach was hard.
The stage was not thought of as a place for nice girls,
and "little people" were treated like children.

So the sisters saved up their money and went home.
By this time, their brother and sisters had moved away
and their parents were very old.
The family house was sadly in need of care,
but it was home
and the sisters loved it.

The two little women worked hard.
They washed the windows.
They swept the floors.
They shined the brass.
They beat dust out of the carpets,

and they turned the house into a tearoom.
During the day they served their guests
with dainty cakes and pots of tea.

At night their home was open to all.
In the summer, lanterns were strung
on the front porch and over the lawn.
Sarah played a little organ,
while Lucy sang gospel songs.
And there were plenty of chairs
for everyone, big and small.

About the Story

This story is based on the lives of Lucy and Sarah Adams, who were real women. They were the only little people in the same Adams family that produced Samuel Adams, who has been called "the father of the American Revolution," and John Quincy Adams, our sixth president.

Born on the island of Martha's Vineyard in 1861, Lucy grew to be forty-nine inches tall. Sarah, who was two and a half years younger, was only forty-six inches. The sisters were discovered by Mrs. Tom Thumb, who read about their performance in a church play. The little women traveled for twenty years with theatrical companies such as Mrs. Thumb's Lilliputian Opera Company and Barnum and Bailey's famous circus. But, deeply religious, the sisters broke with these groups, refusing a European tour because they would not work on Sundays.

The sisters were not limited by their height, nor did they rely on their small size to make them successful as performers. Instead, they studied at performing arts schools in New York, Boston, and Los Angeles to perfect their talents. For thirty years, they produced their own concerts, mostly church programs. They were the only little people to perform on the Chautauqua circuit, which offered traveling programs of lectures and inspirational entertainments.

Although they had suitors, the sisters never married. In 1930, after Sarah was injured in a car accident, they returned to their family home and opened an antiques business and tea garden. Sarah died in 1938, when she was seventy-five, but Lucy, who had a strong spirit as well as good health, lived on to the age of ninety-three.

The sisters' home, built by Eliashib Adams in 1727, still stands off South Road in Chilmark, Massachusetts.